remembering
AMY

The Life and Times of Amy Winehouse

remembering

AMY

The Life and Times of Amy Winehouse

Written by Becky Bowden

PBR

A Pillar Box Red Publication

Contents

Amy Winehouse
Introduction

Amy Winehouse was a Jewish Girl from North London with a passion for music and a voice that was soulful, stunning and instantly recognisable. If ever you heard any of her songs on the radio you would have no doubt that it was Amy Winehouse singing. Her tracks became instant hits and her following knew no bounds.

Radio stations loved her, celebrities wanted to hang out with her and fans just wanted her to continue with the music that she clearly adored making for them.

Despite her often turbulent and fast-paced lifestyle, there was a lot more to Amy than met the eye. She had a soulful voice and a unique style that perfectly encapsulated her rock chick personality and her much loved mix of attitude, star quality and individuality.

Her love-hate relationship with the paparazzi made her one of the most talked about musicians in the media and as a result, her every move was tracked by those keen to get a glimpse into the madness and turmoil that seemed to surround this troubled young star as she made her way through a frenzied and raucous lifestyle.

A musical sensation with a wild side that often contributed to her downfall just as much as it had helped her to succeed in the music business; Amy Winehouse was a rock 'n' roll lifestyle loving star, who sadly never quite managed to deal with the demons of her past.

Tributes

"Amy changed pop music forever, I remember knowing there was hope, and feeling not alone because of her. She lived jazz, she lived the blues."

Lady Gaga

"She was my musical soulmate and like a sister to me. This is one of the saddest days of my life."

Mark Ronson

Amy Winehouse Early Life

Amy Jade Winehouse was born on 14th September 1983 in North London. She spent her early life in and around Southgate where she grew up with her mother, father and older brother Alex.

Life was relatively normal for Amy before she found fame and all of the good and bad things that were brought along with it. Her mother Janis was a pharmacist and her father Mitch worked as a Taxi driver. The couple later separated when Amy was 9 years old but things remained amicable for the children's sake.

Amy would often spend time with her brother, playing his guitar and singing. This led to Amy asking for her own guitar aged just 13, and years of practice definitely seemed to have paid off, as Amy frequently played the guitar at high profile gigs later on in her life.

The whole family shared Amy's love of music and could often be found making their way to theatre shows, concerts and other music events. Her grandmother was even believed to have been romantically involved with the British jazz legend Ronnie Scott. This could have been where Amy's own love of Jazz music came from and how it came to be such a big part of her music, along with soul music and her own unique take on various styles.

Confident in her own ability and her love of music shining through, Amy began to impress friends and family by starting her own girl band called 'Sweet 'n' Sour'. Although this was an amateur band, it was a sign of things to come from Amy as she showed her dedication to music and its various forms. Amy's own personal early musical taste is rumoured to have been in rebellious and confident girl bands like TLC and Salt-N-Pepa. Perhaps this was a clue from a young age that she always had a bit of a wild, independent streak!

When she was 9 years old, Amy's grandmother Cynthia suggested that she attend the Susi Earnshaw Theatre School in order to help her to become better trained and to allow her to fully express her natural musical talent and creativity. She stayed there for four years before being accepted to the highly acclaimed Sylvia Young Theatre School which allowed her to take her musical skill to the next level. It is often claimed that Amy was expelled from the Sylvia Young stage school when she was aged 14 for "not applying herself" but this remains open to speculation as Sylvia Young herself has repeatedly denied this expulsion taking place, stating "She changed schools at 15 - I've heard it said she was expelled; she wasn't. I'd never have expelled Amy." So no-one will ever be completely sure about what exactly happened there, unless some new information comes to light on the issue.

It was as part of the Sylvia Young stage school that Amy Winehouse appeared on an episode of the hit TV show 'The Fast Show' in 1997, alongside regular stars and comedians like Paul Whitehouse, Charlie Higson, Simon Day, Mark Williams, John Thomson, Arabella Weir and Caroline Aherne. This gave Amy and her pals a little taste of life in front of the cameras.

Amy attended the Mount School before going on to enrol at The BRIT School for Performing Arts & Technology. This is the operational name of The London School for Performing Arts & Technology. It is an independent selective technology school partly funded by the BRIT awards located in The Crescent, Selhurst, Croydon, in London, England. It was perfect for a young Amy Winehouse as it is dedicated to education and vocational training for the performing arts, media, art and design and the technologies that make performance possible. Her time here perfecting her skills set her in great stead for things to come in the not too distant future, when her first big break in the music industry would finally come...

Tributes

"The way tears are streaming down my face. Such a loss."

Jessie J

"We have lost a beautiful and talented woman."

Russell Brand

A Life Filled with Music

Amy Winehouse had the best possible start to her career: a supportive family and a great track record. Attending some of the industry's best known and respected stage schools had set her in good footing for the future, and it was only a matter of time before this rising star found her way into the glittering world of stardom.

Amy's big break into the music industry was always on the cards given her natural, raw talent but her first steps into the music world came when her then boyfriend, a guy called Tyler James, sent one of Amy's demo tapes to the A&R division of a record label. These were responsible for talent scouting and overseeing the artistic development of recording artists. Not long after this it came to be that Amy Winehouse was signed to Simon Fuller's '19' management in 2002. Simon is one of the most influential people in the recording industry, having brought us Pop Idol and the various 'Idol' franchises. So this surely meant only good things ahead for a talented Amy's budding career.

Her arrival onto the music scene caused a bit of a stir, with everyone keen to find out who this singer was and where she came from. Music insiders asked around for information, but cards were kept close to the chest until Amy was ready to wow the crowds.

> *"It was as if all the emotions in the universe suddenly were coming out of her mouth."*

Amy had a stage presence that had all of the best talent scouts in a spin, and her soulful style was exactly what the record companies wanted after becoming tired with the same manufactured bands. Her almost nervous, uneasy stage presence became endearing as she was spotted glancing over her shoulder repeatedly at her band members for support, yet her voice was a complete contrast; strong, confident and full of old-style soul.

US music critic Chris Willman summed it up perfectly when he gushed, "It was as if all the emotions in the universe suddenly were coming out of her mouth."

Major record label Island Records soon got wind that there was a new artist in town and were blown away by Amy's talent. They quickly signed her, and this is where she remained for the rest of her career.

On 20th October 2003, Amy released her debut album 'Frank' which was mostly produced by hip hop producer Salaam Remi. The album had a heavy jazz influence and Amy once again showed her talent as both a writer and performer by co-writing all but two of the songs on this album.

The album did well, making Amy a great starting point to build from and getting her name out there. She was compared to the likes of other female singers with distinctive voices such as Macy Gray and Sarah Vaughan.

> *"I really started writing music to challenge myself, to see what I could write; I felt there was nothing new that was coming out that really represented me and the way I felt. So I started writing my own stuff."*

People quickly began to know who she was and her fan base grew by the day. Everyone saw Amy as this cool, offbeat performer who just oozed her own unique charm, and everyone wanted a piece of her.

The album 'Frank' was praised by judges when it won the Mercury Prize in 2004. They hailed it as "an ebullient blend of raw emotions, sardonic sensibilities and an original take on jazz and R&B."

That same year saw the album nominated at the Brit Awards for "British Female Solo Artist" and "British Urban Act", and Amy Winehouse continued to have the year of her life when she was awarded the prestigious Ivor Novello songwriting award for "Best Contemporary Song", along with Salaam Remi.

After a string of successful festival appearances, winning awards and various other high profile events and publicity tours, Amy Winehouse was beginning to become a household name!

The next album to be released was 'Back to Black' which is probably the one that everyone really remembers her for in the mainstream music world. With a lot of help from her friend and fellow musician Mark Ronson who co-produced the album alongside Salaam Remi, Winehouse released 'Back to Black' helping her hit even newer heights in her now meteoric rise to fame.

The challenge for Amy during her career was always to keep true to herself and to continue to write music that she felt represented her and her style. She said in a BBC interview, "I really started writing music to challenge myself, to see what I could write; I felt there was nothing new that was coming out that really represented me and the way I felt. So I started writing my own stuff."

'Back to Black' went to number 1 in the UK music charts and became the best-selling album of the year with an outstanding 1.85 million copies sold. Amy was hitting heights that other artists could only dream of, but were her partying antics that came with fame and fortune about to take their toll on the singer?

Following Amy Winehouse's death, millions of fans bought 'Back to Black' making it the number 2 bestseller in the iTunes charts. This represented a bittersweet tribute to a singer who would be sorely missed.

Dionne Bromfield

Amy's love of music knew no bounds; she was forever singing and writing her own tracks. It came as no surprise to those in the industry when Amy decided to launch her own record label, the quirkily titled 'Lioness Records'.

Her first signing was none other than Dionne Bromfield; a close family friend and Amy's goddaughter. Born on February 1st, 1996 Dionne Bromfield is a soul singer/songwriter from London whose own vocal talent wowed Amy and others in the industry. She has a reputation for being one of the most polite and hugely talented young musicians on the music scene right now and her career has

gone from strength to strength during her time in the public eye with Amy.

It was on 20th July 2011 that Dionne was performing at London's Roundhouse with hit boy band The Wanted when much to fans delight she was joined on stage by her godmother, Amy Winehouse. It was unknown to everyone at the time that this would be Winehouse's last public performance before her death on 23rd July 2011, aged 27.

Dionne often refers to Amy as her mentor, and there is no doubt that her success has been helped not only by her own amazing, soulful edgy voice but also from continued support from Amy Winehouse along the way. Amy frequently showed her protective, nurturing side when around Dionne, and their bond was apparent to anyone who saw them together. Since learning of her godmother's death, Dionne has announced that she would be cancelling all public appearances and media commitments until further notice. She was quoted on her official website as saying, "I'm totally devastated... Amy was my inspiration."

Here you can find a brief Amy Winehouse Discography featuring her best hits. Have you got them all in your collection?

Discography

Albums

Frank - Universal Island Records 2003

Back To Black - Island Records Group 2006

Absolutely Live (CD-ROM) - Not On Label 2007

Frank & Back To Black (4xCD Box Set) - Island Records Group, Universal Records 2008

Singles & EPs

Frank (Album Sampler) - Universal Island Records 2003

Stronger Than Me - Island Records 2003

Take The Box - Island Records 2004

Pumps / Help Yourself - Universal Island Records 2004

In My Bed / You Sent Me Flying - Universal Island Records 2004

You Know I'm No Good - Universal Island Records 2006

Rehab - Universal Island Records 2006

Valerie Baby J Remix - Mark Ronson featuring Amy Winehouse - Sony BMG Music Entertainment (UK) Ltd. 2007

Don't Stop The Music / You Know I'm No Good - Rihanna / Amy Winehouse - Universal Music México, S.A. de C.V. 2007

Tears Dry On Their Own - Universal Island Records 2007

Love Is A Losing Game - Universal Island Records 2007

Back To Black - Universal Island Records 2007

Frank - Remixes - Island Records 2007

My Destructive Side (12") - Vinni MC & Amy Winehouse – Lioness Records 2009

"Can't quite get my head round the news about Amy, such a talent, such a sad day, such a loss. RIP Amy x."

Edith Bowman

"Such desperately sad news re Amy Winehouse. Supreme talent, terrible self-destructive addictive personality."

Piers Morgan

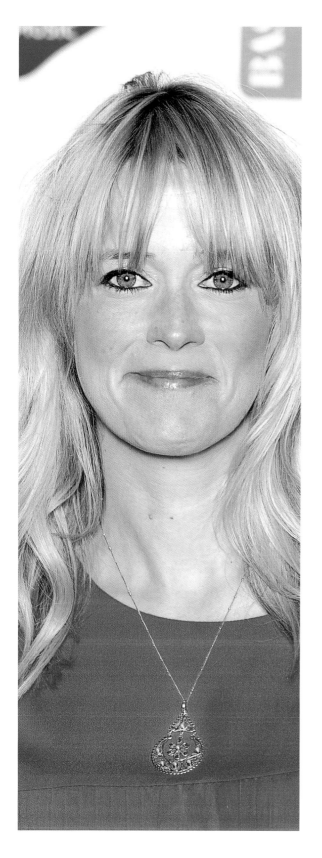

Amy Winehouse Live on Stage

The 'Back to Black' singer had her fair share of live performances throughout her career. There were the good, the bad and the downright shambolic! We take a look back at some of Amy's live on stage highlights marking the most notable performances from her musical career. Take a look at some of the highlights and the unfortunate lowest moments in pictures as we recall Amy Winehouse live on stage during her turbulent musical career.

V Festival 2004

Amy's performance at the much loved V Festival in 2004 was one of the first big performances of her career. Thanks to the success of her first album, 'Frank', the 2004 V Festival performance showed Amy at her early, wonderfully vulnerable best with no interest in showing off on stage or acting up, she simply came to perform and do what she loved best. This was the Amy that fans first fell in love with.

Prince's Trust Urban Music Festival 2004

Amy would go on to perform on the first day of the Prince's Trust Urban Music Festival in 2004, a perfect fit for this cute and quirky musical star. She looked naturally beautiful and wore a simplistic but stylish outfit, and we once again saw a glimpse of this raw, edgy talent.

Shepherd's Bush Empire 2004

2004 was certainly Amy's year as she was high in demand on the gigs and tours list! She performed at Shepherd's Bush Empire on 3rd May 2004. She wore a figure hugging dress, showing her at her most healthy and a far cry from the fragile looking star she was later to become.

Brits 2007

In 2007 Amy donned her trademark beehive and strappy dress to perform 'Rehab' at the Brits. She arrived on stage to booming applause and supportive chants from the crowd. She appeared cool and confident, with a sophisticated edge.

MTV Awards 2007

It is reported that 'Die Hard' actor and fan Bruce Willis specifically requested to introduce Winehouse on stage before her performance of 'Rehab' at the 2007 MTV Movie Awards. Winehouse apparently made awards organisers nervous when she went on a Las Vegas jaunt just a few hours before the show.

G-A-Y 2007

Amy performed at G-A-Y in 2007 sporting her tussled beehive, tight jeans and a white strappy top. She showed off her tattoos on her arms and strutted her stuff on stage, looking like she was having fun!

Shepherd's Bush Empire 2007

Performing at Shepherd's Bush Empire on 28th May 2007 Amy was beginning to look frailer. She wore a retro style dress with an oversized black belt, her oversized lightning bolt tattoo clearly visible as she raised her mic to sing.

Isle of Wight Festival 2007

The Isle of Wight Festival performance in 2007 saw Amy Winehouse perform tracks including her classic 'Me and Mr Jones', she frequently flipped her hair and adjusted her beehive as she sang to the crowds.

Glastonbury 2007

Amy was invited to play her classic track 'Rehab' to the millions of fans flocking the fields of Glastonbury Festival in 2007. She wore a green strappy top and her usual dramatic eye makeup seemed thicker and more heavily applied than ever.

Mercury Prize 2007

Despite being beaten to an award by The Klaxons, Amy attended the Mercury Music Awards in 2007 and was accused of 'stealing the show' by many music insiders.

Brits 2008

On 20th February 2008 Amy gave a classic performance at The Brit Awards, she performed alongside Mark Ronson singing the track 'Valerie' followed by 'Love is a Losing Game' and famously urged the crowd to "Make some noise for my Blake."

Mandela's 90th 2008

The star looked frail and pale as she performed at Mandela's 90th birthday concert in 2008. However she got through her set without any major hitches.

Glastonbury 2008

Amy returned to the legendary Glastonbury Festival in 2008 for a repeat performance. She was reported to have been confident and interacted well with her fans, running to the front of the stage to high five and clasp hands with some as she sang. The singer performed a wide variety of songs from her albums to a cheering crowd.

T in the Park 2008

Despite fears of a 'no show', Amy appeared at T in the Park in 2008 wearing an outfit with a distinctive rock edge and performing a 14-song set.

V Festival 2008

Amy appeared gaunt and frail during her appearance at V Festival in 2008. She wore a chequer outfit and seemed far from the Amy we had seen in earlier career performances.

Rock in Rio 2008

Amy's set at Rock in Rio 2008 was plagued with problems. She arrived late and later had problems with her voice. This added to the public speculation that all was not well with the troubled star.

Comeback Show Brazil 2011

Amy played five dates in a comeback tour in Brazil in 2011. Reactions from the crowds were mixed.

Serbia

Amy was allegedly behaving erratically in a gig in Serbia close to the end of her life and was repeatedly booed by fans. This was widely reported in the press as the stories of Amy's further deterioration hit the newspapers.

Last Performance

Amy's final performance of her career was in Camden's Roundhouse, London on 20th July 2011, when she surprised guests by making a shock appearance on stage to support her goddaughter, Dionne Bromfield, who was singing 'Mama Said' with The Wanted. The singers both apparently received warm applause from the audience.

Tributes

"I just really hope that she's found peace now wherever she is."

Carole King

"It's a very sad loss of a very good friend I spent many great times with."

Ronnie Wood

Love, Relationships and Marriage

Love, Relationships and Marriage

Amy Winehouse had several high profile relationships during the course of her career. Here we take a look back at some of the most highly publicised and those that really had an effect on her life, for better and for worse.

Tyler James

Tyler James is a musician from Barnsley, South Yorkshire who dated Amy in the early stages of her career. He guested on an R&B track titled 'Wilder' which turned out to be very popular in the nightclubs in and around London. Due to the success of this track, Tyler began touring around pubs and clubs locally and gained a good musical following. In 2002 he was even hailed as "The New Justin Timberlake" by The Face Magazine.

It is believed that Tyler was actually the person who helped Amy break into the industry, sending some of her music to an A&R person.

Alex Clare

Winehouse dated this multi-talented musician in 2006. A fellow London-based composer, singer, songwriter and once part-time chef, he is now signed to the same label as Amy Winehouse; Island Records. The relationship didn't end well for Amy and Alex, with Alex famously selling his story to The News of the World newspaper, who published a very risqué piece about the couple and their antics in the bedroom and beyond. The now infamous feature titled "Bondage Crazed Amy Just Can't Beehive in Bed" was released and did nothing to help Amy's already rapidly deteriorating public image.

Blake Fielder-Civil

Blake and Amy began their bittersweet and somewhat rocky relationship by a meeting of chance.

Blake Fielder-Civil recalls, "We met at a pub called the Good Mixer. I'd just had a good win at the bookies so I went to the pub to celebrate, opened the door and Amy was the first person I saw and that was it," he told the Daily Mail newspaper. "And from that night onwards, we began our tortuous love affair. The drinks were on me for the first and last time!"

The road of 'true love' was anything but smooth for the couple and Blake was repeatedly accused by paparazzi and concerned friends and family of being the one who introduced Amy to the world of Class A drugs.

The couple briefly split in 2006 when Blake left Amy and got back together with an ex-girlfriend. Amy was left heartbroken and it was during this time that she began work on her album 'Back to Black' which had a decidedly more sombre tone to it. The album enjoyed huge success, with Amy pouring her heartbreak into her lyrics.

It was a year later that Amy and Blake found themselves once more reunited and their destructive love affair continued down its bumpy path of passion and pain.

In April 2007 Amy and Blake announced that they had become engaged. Amy spoke to The Sun newspaper and gave the following quote regarding her decision to marry Blake:

"He proposed to me at home a few days ago and I took a day to finally agree. Obviously we are both young and it is frightening. But it is the right thing to do. That is why I agreed."

The two certainly didn't waste any time tying the knot, as just a few weeks later they wed in a surprise ceremony in Miami, Florida. Later that year they were both arrested in Bergen, Norway on charges of possession of Marijuana but escaped with a fine. This would be a sign of more troubled times to come. As word quickly spread and more people worried about Amy and Blake's influence on each other, their tumultuous relationship spiralled further out of control.

The couple entered rehab in early August 2007 where they spent a brief time before checking themselves out, supposedly to "go and buy a guitar". They were later spotted

"He proposed to me at home a few days ago and I took a day to finally agree. Obviously we are both young and it is frightening. But it is the right thing to do. That is why I agreed."

by the paparazzi covered in matching bruises and scratches which Amy would later go on to explain were a part of their violent and often drug fuelled history together.

When Blake was imprisoned for an incident involving trying to bribe a witness, Amy found a brief glimpse of happiness in Josh Bowman, an up and coming young actor. She appears to have come to her senses and is quoted as saying that the "whole marriage was based on doing drugs" and that "for the time being I've just forgotten I'm even married," with regards to her relationship with Blake.

Blake filed for divorce from prison and after a brief period of Amy being reluctant to sign the papers, stating "I still love my Blake. I won't let him divorce me," continuing "Blake is the male version of me. We're perfect for each other. I don't want to go back home to England. I want to wait for Blake here," the couple officially divorced in 2009 and Blake received no money from the divorce settlement.

However, the couple were spotted hanging out together in 2010, fuelling rumours that maybe their relationship had once again been rekindled.

Reg Traviss

Closest to the time of her death, Amy Winehouse was reported to be dating British film director Reg Traviss. The couple were said to have been happy together and since Amy's death there have been rumours that Reg had even given Amy an engagement ring, asking her to marry him.

Reg Traviss expressed his state of shock and grief to The Sun newspaper days after the star's death.

"Amy kept trying to decide what to wear," he told the paper. "She had laid out her dresses to make up her mind. She was really looking forward to it.

"She has been full of life and so upbeat recently, exercising everyday and doing yoga. This terrible thing that happened is like an accident."

He went on to add:

"The last three days have been hell. We have suffered a terrible untimely loss and want peace now.

"I can't describe what I am going through and I want to thank so much all of the people who have paid their respects and who are mourning the loss of Amy, such a beautiful, brilliant person and my dear love. I have lost my darling who I loved very much."

There is no doubt that Amy's relationships were turbulent to say the least, but this troubled young singer poured her heart and soul into each of them, maybe giving too much of herself and her own personality up in the process.

"I can't describe what I am going through and I want to thank so much all of the people who have paid their respects and who are mourning the loss of Amy, such a beautiful, brilliant person and my dear love. I have lost my darling who I loved very much."

Tributes

"She paved the way for artists like me and made people excited about British music again."

Adele

"Devastated. I spent extraordinary times with Amy. She sang for me once for hours, it was the most beautiful & touching thing. A huge loss."

Dita Von Teese

An Unforgettable Style!

If there's one thing that is certain about Amy Winehouse, it is that she definitely wasn't afraid to express her own sense of style! Amy knew what she liked and the look she wanted to achieve and wore it with confidence and attitude.

It was her trademark 'Beehive' hairdo that first caught people's eye when she made her way onto the music scene. Everyone was talking about this edgy new singer with the coolest 'rock chick' look and a sixties pin-up style edge. With the voice to match, it was no wonder Amy began to gain a cult following so quickly.

Amy's stylist Alex Foden was said to have borrowed the beehive hairstyle and her Cleopatra style striking eye makeup from one of Amy's favourite bands The Ronettes, who were a popular 1960s girl group from New York City. Her style so closely resembled that of Ronnie Spector that the Ronettes singer is said to have exclaimed "I don't know her, I never met her, and when I saw that pic, I thought, 'That's me!' But then I found out, no, it's Amy! I didn't have on my glasses," when talking about having seen Amy in a picture.

Amy had a wide range of tattoos, having gotten her first proper tattoo at the tender age of 15. The tattoos ranged from images of pin-up girls, a lightning bolt, feathers and a large horseshoe on her left upper arm. One of her more recent tattoos was a large American eagle behind a stars-and-stripes ankh cross. The Egyptian hieroglyph of the ankh cross holds the meaning of eternal life.

Many other celebrities have tattooed this ankh image on themselves, including Shaquille O'Neal, Erykah Badu and Dennis Rodman.

Just a month after Amy and ex-husband Blake Fielder-Civil started dating in 2005 Amy decided to get a tattoo just above her breast, over her heart saying "Blake's". Her mother Janis had many words to say about her disapproval of Amy's tattoos, quoted in The Daily Mail as saying: "That dreadful one saying "Blake's" on her breast - I hate that. It was like when Amy got her Daddy's Girl tattoo. She asked me, 'Do you want me to get mummy tattooed, too?' I said, 'No, don't worry'. That's not my thing."

Headscarves, oversized hooped earrings and bright red lips all became something that Amy would be seen sporting on a regular basis. She wore a stunning selection of forties, fifties and sixties inspired tops and dresses during her early career and even caught the eye of fashion guru Karl Lagerfeld. He apparently came to see Amy as something of a muse and drew inspiration from her style for one of his collections. So much so that during the Chanel runway show in 2007, many of the models walked the runway with Amy's eye-catching trademark beehive hair.

At the time of the show, Karl Lagerfeld himself declared, "She's a style icon," when speaking about Amy Winehouse and his love of her distinct look.

> *"We had a great working and personal relationship with Amy during the design and development of the collaboration. Amy's unique sense of style and attitude pervaded the entire collection. She was a pleasure to work with and will be deeply missed by the entire Fred Perry team."*

The question on everyone in the fashion industry's lips right now must be whether Amy's unseen fashion designs will ever be released to the public? The musical star had been working with Fred Perry to create a clothing line that represented her style and released some of the early collection from her range in Autumn 2010.

Talking about the prospect of working with such a high profile fashion name, Amy said, "I knew exactly what I wanted, and I love Fred Perry so much. I was honoured that they would even ask, like, 'Do you want to come and do a line?' Me? Like, me?"

It has become public knowledge since her death that she had an amazing amount of finished designs still to be released. Does this mean that perhaps Amy may do the impossible and finish her clothing line from beyond the grave? A spokesperson told The Daily Mail, "Everything is on hold until we speak with Amy's family and management." So who knows what could happen down the line? They went on to issue the following statement:

"We had a great working and personal relationship with Amy during the design and development of the collaboration, Amy's unique sense of style and attitude pervaded the entire collection. She was a pleasure to work with and will be deeply missed by the entire Fred Perry team."

Despite her style triumphs, Amy hasn't always been the height of fashion! Some of you will remember her various fashion disasters when she became troubled by addiction and various personal issues. The star was often snapped by paparazzi out and about looking bleary eyed and half dressed. She was once snapped by paparazzi as she wandered aimlessly outside her London home in just her jeans and a bright red bra, a shot that has come to be well-known for showing Amy at one of her lowest moments.

Her trademark beehive at times became non-existent or completely dishevelled and her clothes were either hanging from her body awkwardly or had become drab and uninspiring. It was a heart-breaking time for Amy Winehouse fans as they saw the singer that they loved descend into a shadow of her former self. There would be many instances of this on and off throughout Amy's career and times when she would once again appear to be back to her bright and breezy self only to fall once more at the next hurdle.

Everyone wanted more than anything for Amy to regain that spark and sparkle of her early career and at times it looked as though that was also what Amy wanted as she worked towards rehab and beating her troubles once and for all, battling on and off with the addictions that had taken such a hold on her life. Unfortunately Amy's time was cut tragically short, but her look and appearance will always be remembered as iconic, unique and a real rock 'n' roll style siren that pushed the fashion boundaries.

Tributes

"It's just beyond sad, there's nothing else to say. She was such a lost soul, may she rest in peace."

Lily Allen

"RIP Amy Winehouse. So sad to see such a talent gone and her life end in tragedy. This makes me terribly sad."

LeAnn Rimes

Amy's Battle with Addiction

Amy Winehouse was a musical legend, there is no doubt about that. However, one of the things that frustrated her fans and family most was watching the star battle with her addiction to drink and drugs. It was a long, seemingly un-ending fight for Amy as she frequently declared she was turning her life around, only to be spotted out and about with her actions painting quite a different picture.

Those who knew Amy best spoke of her love for people and her friends and family. They talked about the 'real' Amy that perhaps we, the public, weren't always privy to as much as we would have liked. Instead, a lot of us were left with a picture of Amy that suggested that the star's life revolved only around the party lifestyle. This is something that as time passes after her death we learn not to be entirely true.

As with any addiction battle, especially one so heavily featured in the public eye, Amy would experience regular lows and moments of desperation as she continued down what some viewed as a path to self-destruction.

As a result of her addictions, Amy developed respiratory conditions including one that could lead to early stage emphysema, which is a long-term, progressive disease of the lungs that primarily causes shortness of breath due to over-inflation of the alveoli (the air sacs in the lung). In people suffering from emphysema, the lung tissue involved in exchange of gases, oxygen and carbon dioxide, is impaired or destroyed.

Her father Mitch Winehouse was quoted at the time as saying that his daughter's lungs were operating at 70 percent capacity and that she had an irregular heartbeat. Amy was admitted for treatment but was later controversially snapped by the paps smoking a cigarette, a shot that ultimately caused upset with a lot of fellow sufferers of the same condition and only fuelled the public's annoyance at what some felt to be the musician's unwillingness to help herself.

On 7th May 2008, Amy Winehouse was jailed after she was caught on video smoking what appeared to be crack cocaine. She was released on bail after only a few hours as it could not be 100% confirmed from the video exactly what the substance was that she was smoking. She was later arrested again on 19th December 2009 when she assaulted the front of house manager at a Milton Keynes theatre when he asked her to move from her seat.

On 20th January 2010, Winehouse admitted common assault and disorderly behaviour and was ordered to pay court costs, give compensation to the man she attacked and was given a two year conditional discharge.

Some celebrities aired their rising concerns for the state of the musician's health as she continued to gain awards for her work whilst news of her addiction raged in the public news. Natalie Cole, daughter of Jazz legend Nat King Cole who introduced Amy Winehouse on stage at the prestigious Grammy's award ceremony in 2008 said, "I think the girl is talented, gifted, but it's not right for her to be able to have her cake and eat it too. She needs to get herself together." – Cole has also battled her own addictions in previous years.

Other celebrities also said their piece about Amy's addiction, with friend Lily Allen saying in an interview with Scotland on Sunday, "I know Amy Winehouse very well. And she is

very different to what people portray her as being. Yes, she does get out of her mind on drugs sometimes, but she is also a very clever, intelligent, witty, funny person who can hold it together. You just don't see that side."

Pained by his daughter's sudden death, father Mitch Winehouse has since attended a Westminster meeting with chairman of the Home Affairs Select Committee, Keith Vaz, and Home Office minister James Brokenshire to urge politicians to do more to help young people with drug and alcohol problems. He

took with him into the meeting an addiction expert, Sarah Graham, who commented, "We are looking at how we can fund a rehab in Amy's name but we don't think the foundation should pay for it. If we build something, we need the Government to commit to pay for the beds long-term."

Amy's father publically spoke out about the lack of help for young people fighting their own battles with addiction saying:

"This isn't about Amy because we were in a fortunate position of being able to fund Amy to go into private rehab – this is about people that can't afford it."

Britain's only NHS rehabilitation centre for young people, Middlegate, in Lincolnshire, closed last year, leaving young addicts facing either waits of up to two years for NHS treatment or large bills at private clinics. Mr Winehouse said: "Rather than money being wasted through the criminal justice system, there could be a reallocation of funds."

Ironically, in the weeks leading up to her death, Amy's father Mitch revealed in a statement that she "was the happiest she'd been for years." At a private ceremony Mitch indicated that she had just finished three weeks of abstinence when she passed away and was ready to embrace a clean slate. "She said, 'Dad, I've had enough of drinking. I can't stand the look on your and the family's faces anymore.'"

"She said, 'Dad, I've had enough of drinking. I can't stand the look on your and the family's faces anymore.'"

Tributes

"Poor Amy. She was a great guest on Buzzcocks, funny + outrageous. And a great talent. What a terrible waste."

Bill Bailey

"i cant even breathe right now im crying so hard i just lost 1 of my best friends. i love you forever Amy & will never forget the real you!"

Kelly Osbourne

*Celebrity Friends
and Influences*

Celebrity Friends and Influences

Amy Winehouse was no stranger to the celebrity scene. Over the course of her short career she managed to gain quite a following with fellow celebrities, musicians and stars. Everyone knew her name and many wanted to hang out with her after hearing about her partying antics and crazy nights out.

Friends of Amy Winehouse have been keen to tell of the person they felt she really was since her passing, with a lot of celebrities and stars taking to their various websites and social media platforms and making statements to the press about their time together. We see a picture of Amy emerging that shows us more about the star's life, her friends in the celebrity scene and how her life was filled with so much more than the highly publicised addiction and troubles that we had come to associate her with.

Alex Foden

Amy Winehouse was close friends with her stylist Alex Foden and the two were often snapped out and about together by paparazzi. Alex was always keen to try and keep the star's image in check, picking out clothing and styles that reflected her true personality, and although he couldn't be there 24/7 to handle the star's much publicised wardrobe malfunctions at times, he did a great job of her styling especially in the early years of her career when she was first starting to make an impression on the public and the media. Alex made sure she was always dressed to impress and that everyone got a glimpse of her love for jazz and soul through her outfits.

The two became inseparable as they continued to work together, often supporting each other in times of need.

It was clear that the people in Amy's inner circle had an entirely different perception of her than the one of the public. Alex Foden was quoted as saying "All she wanted was to start a family and open a singing school - the price of fame was hard for Amy" during an interview with Radio 5 live.

He added his views on her rocky relationship with Blake Fielder-Civil saying of the couple's strong bond that he witnessed:

"That can never be taken away and that was quite clear to see.

"Nobody can describe to you that feeling unless they have been that dangerously in love.

"Her and Blake were thick as thieves, she loved him. It was everybody else that didn't and the same with me and Blake, Amy surrounded herself with people that were not good for her."

Zalon Thompson

Zalon Thompson, close friend and backing singer to Amy spoke up and added:

"She actually wasn't really interested in the whole celebrity world. She was more into being a housewife singing in bars and thinking about children." Further alluding to that side of Amy that the public certainly wasn't aware of.

Mark Ronson

Mark Ronson was a close personal friend to Amy Winehouse and not only thought of her as a little sister, but collaborated with her on various projects and helped produce an album 'Back to Black' for her. The two struck up a great friendship, with Ronson often praising the star and her talent. The two did have their fair share of falling out from time to time, most notably when Amy decided to pretend to kiss him in front of the Paparazzi on a night out. The musician angrily ranted to Virgin Radio, frustrated with Amy for playing games with the press and jeopardising his relationship with his girlfriend.

"She actually wasn't really interested in the whole celebrity world. She was more into being a housewife singing in bars and thinking about children."

The 'Valerie' DJ revealed he was angered by her publicity stunt where she pretended to kiss him at the K West Hotel, in Notting Hill.

Mark told presenters on Virgin Radio: "I didn't think it was very funny to tell you the truth. I was like, 'my girlfriend's parents are going to read that in the paper in the morning'. I guess I'm just not as aware of the games that go on with the paparazzi."

The two never seemed to be angry for long though and regularly went on to collaborate more and remained close friends. Mark dedicated one of his shows to her just after having attended her funeral and seemed completely devastated by the loss of someone so close to him.

Kelly Osbourne

Kelly Osbourne was a close female friend of Amy Winehouse, it is unclear how the two met and became friends but perhaps given that they moved in similar circles and both have a previous history with addiction this could have been a shared bonding point.

After her friend's death, Kelly had tweeted about how much she missed her and how devastated she was. She attended Amy's funeral wearing her long blonde hair in her friend's trademark beehive style hairdo, pink lips and dark glasses.

Aisleyne Horgan-Wallace

Former reality TV Show 'Big Brother' contestant Aisleyne Horgan-Wallace struck up an unlikely friendship with Amy Winehouse around three years prior to her death. Aisleyne was pictured outside the star's London home shortly after her death was announced where she appeared to break down in tears, curling into a ball on the floor, looking inconsolable to friends who had accompanied her.

"It's devastating. I'm heartbroken anyway, losing Amy. I just want her back. But to have this thrown at me, and all the internet hate that I'm getting now. The messages have been just vile and it's hard because it's not true. There's not a scrap of truth in it."

She later appeared on 'This Morning' TV show and spoke about her reaction to her friend's death and the negative comments she had received in regards to her friendship with Amy as well as her strong emotional reaction to hearing the news of her passing.

Aisleyne told 'This Morning' hosts Eamonn Holmes and Ruth Langsford:

"A certain journalist said that I was seen with her a few days before... he also said that I need to ask myself what I was thinking, being in that situation with Amy when she was perhaps quite fragile.

"The papers are saying the last time I was with her we were drinking. In fact the last time I was with her was in her house, in her kitchen, we were drinking tea and having a girlie gossip as I would with any friend. Just talking about guys."

She continued her tearful interview saying:

"It's devastating. I'm heartbroken anyway, losing Amy. I just want her back. But to have this thrown at me, and all the internet hate that I'm getting now. The messages have been just vile and it's hard because it's not true. There's not a scrap of truth in it."

Speaking of how she was supportive of Amy's long running battle to beat her addictions she finished the interview by stating:

"She got herself completely well and she did the impossible, which was to get clean. I'm just so proud of her for getting past it and overcoming it. She did the impossible as I say and she really did."

Pete Doherty

Amy struck up a seemingly bizarre friendship with cult band Babyshambles frontman Pete Doherty in the years leading up to her death, with Amy apparently even offering Pete a place to stay in her London home.

Friends worried that the two would be bad for each other, given both of their past history with drug use and addiction in its various forms, but Amy thought that she could help Pete out; she thought a lot of him.

Amy's father Mitch was not so keen however, branding the pale-faced male singer a "scumbag" in a comment at the time. Much to her family's relief, Amy and Pete's friendship seemed to have been a lot less intense over the last year or two, with Amy not having supported Pete during his imprisonment in 2008 and choosing instead to get on with her own life.

Tributes

"Truly sad news about Amy Winehouse. My heart goes out to her family. May her troubled soul find peace."

Demi Moore

"Just heard the shocking news of Amy Winehouse's death. Absolutely tragic. Such a talented artist. So sad."

Jay Sean

Amy Winehouse's Death

Amy Jade Winehouse passed away suddenly and unexpectedly at her London home on 23rd July 2011. At just 27 years old, the troubled musician was an iconic British talent with a unique and soulful voice that will forever be remembered by fans and all of those in the music industry who ever worked with her.

Krissi Murison, editor of NME who had interviewed Winehouse many times, summed up the loss of this much loved musical talent perfectly, commenting on how the singer's impact on British music would continue to be felt for many years. She said "Her influence has been phenomenal and I think we absolutely will remember her as one of the British pop greats alongside artists like Dusty Springfield," She clearly opened the door for lots of other female artists. She was a jazz singer but it was soul, her soul, in her lyrics that meant that it didn't matter what kind of music you were in to – you couldn't help but be moved."

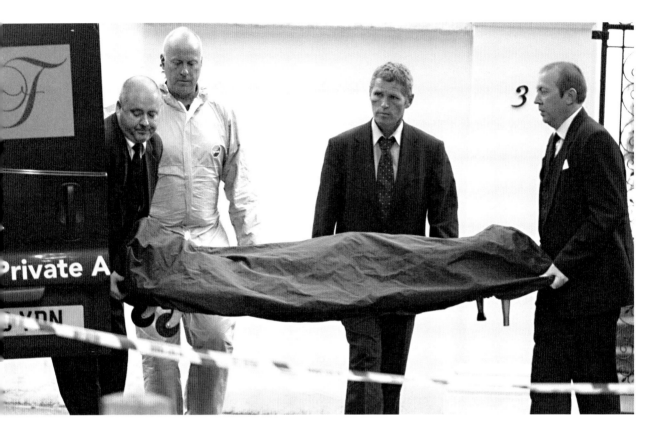

Amy's body was reportedly found at around 3:54 on Saturday 23rd July by her bodyguard, Ray Grange, who called the police immediately. Her family were then notified and gave the following statement upon hearing the heart-breaking news:

"Our family has been left bereft by the loss of Amy, a wonderful daughter, sister, niece. She leaves a gaping hole in our lives.

"We are coming together to remember her and we would appreciate some privacy and space at this terrible time."

An initial police statement on Saturday evening read:

"Police were called by London Ambulance Service to an address in Camden Square NW1 shortly before 16.05hrs today, Saturday 23 July, following reports of a woman found deceased.

"On arrival officers found the body of a 27-year-old female who was pronounced dead at the scene.

"Enquiries continue into the circumstances of the death."

"Our family has been left bereft by the loss of Amy, a wonderful daughter, sister, niece. She leaves a gaping hole in our lives."

Amy's mum Janis saw her daughter the day before she died and is glad that she got to hear her daughter tell her, "I love you, mum" before they parted. "They are the words I will always treasure. I'm glad I saw her when I did," Janis said. She went on to add that during the visit, "she seemed out of it."

Amy's father, Mitch, reportedly cancelled all of his commitments and took a flight home from New York City where he had a scheduled performance. Mitch reportedly said, "I'm getting on the next plane back. I'm coming home. I have to be with Amy, I can't crack up for her sake. My family needs me. I'm devastated; it's such a shock."

Meanwhile fans began to gather outside the star's home, leaving tributes in the form of flowers, soft toys, cards, messages and some even left cans of alcohol and brought their own, sat down together and raised their glasses in a toast to the star in a bizarre but perhaps seemingly fitting tribute in some fans' eyes.

People flocked to the singer's home over the next few days after her passing; they were often spoken to by members of Amy's own family who came out to look at the hundreds of tributes that had been paid. Amy's father, Mitch, said to them, "I can't tell you what this means to us. It really is making this a lot easier." He was pictured giving fans some of Amy's own clothes on one occasion outside her home, stating, "These are Amy's t-shirts; this is what she would have wanted, for her fans to have her clothes." As he left the house, he added: "God bless Amy Winehouse."

Fans later put on the t-shirts and stopped to pose for paparazzi pictures which later emerged on the front pages of national newspapers.

"Goodnight my angel ... Sleep tight. Mommy and Daddy love you ever so much."

Amy Winehouse's funeral was held on Tuesday 26th July 2011 at Edgwarebury cemetery in north London. Afterwards Amy's body was taken to the Golders Green crematorium; this was reportedly where her beloved grandmother was cremated. Family then made their way to Schindler Hall in Southgate to mark the beginning of a 'shiva' which is a traditional period of mourning in Amy's family's Jewish faith.

During the funeral service Mitch paid a heartfelt and touching tribute to his daughter, ending with the heart-breaking words, "Goodnight my angel ... Sleep tight. Mommy and Daddy love you ever so much."

The service was given by a Rabbi (a close family friend) in both Hebrew and English.

The funeral reportedly ended with the mourners singing "So Far Away" by Carole King, one of Amy's favourite songs. The lyrics read, "Holding you again could only do me good, oh how I wish I could, but you're so far away." A sad reflection of how everyone close to Amy must have been feeling at this terrible time.

There were many family and friends in attendance, including some of Amy's closest celebrity pals. Singer and fellow rock chick Kelly Osbourne paid a touching tribute to her much loved friend by styling her long blonde hair into a beehive, fixed with an oversized black bow headband and a simple, elegant black dress with black wedged heels. Friend and musical collaborator Mark Ronson arrived looking dapper and clean cut in a black suit and everyone appeared to be banding together, looking respectful and supportive. The atmosphere was reported to be calm and cool.

The 27 Club

Amy Winehouse's passing at the age of 27 has now stirred up much media hype about the infamous '27 Club'. This refers to a group of musicians whose lives were all cut tragically short aged just 27 years old, with Amy becoming their latest sad addition. Many of them had also battled addiction in various forms, including drink and drugs.

Other members of the so-called '27 Club' include:

Jim Morrisson, Janis Joplin, Robert Johnson, Brian Jones, Kurt Cobain, Jimi Hendrix and now Winehouse along with some other less familiar names from the music scene.

But look beyond the glamorous picture painted of the so-called 27 Club, or the 'curse of 27' as it is often referred and you will find a series of sad, addiction-ravaged lives that could have ended so much differently. There's nothing to be proud of in this club and it is most certainly not 'cool' as the media often likes to portray. Amy was sadly a kindred spirit to these fellow stars, with a wild lifestyle and a rebellious attitude that often caused her more trouble than it did good. She will always be remembered for her stunning, soulful voice and the classic songs that have made an impact on the British music industry and millions of fans over her short but fast-paced life.

RIP Amy Winehouse, you will be missed by many.

Tributes

"It's not age that Hendrix, Jones, Joplin, Morrison, Cobain & Amy have in common - it's drug abuse, sadly."

Billy Bragg

"Amy Winehouse found dead at her home. So very very sad. A huge talent."

Davina McCall

Tributes

"Times like this remind me why it's so important to live life to the fullest!! Amy Winehouse you will be a LEGEND in all our hearts!"

JLS

"I really hope she's at peace now. I don't wanna hear any chat about it's her own fault, addiction is a powerful demon."

Professor Green

ISBN 978 1 907823 21 3

Picture credits:

Front cover: Eddie van der Walt
p2: Myung Jung Kim/PA Archive/Press Association Images
p4: Yui Mok/PA Archive/Press Association Images
Suzan/EMPICS Entertainment
Joel Ryan/PA Archive/Press Association Images
p7: Matt Dunham/AP/Press Association Images
p8-9: Suzan/EMPICS Entertainment
p11: Guibbaud-Orban/ABACA/Press Association Images
Justin Goff/UK Press/Press Association Images
p13: 90078/CBI/DPA/Press Association Images
p14: Andy Butterton/PA Archive/Press Association Images
p15: Myung Jung Kim/PA Archive/Press Association Images
p17: Ian West/PA Wire/Press Association Images
Suzan/EMPICS Entertainment
p19: Yui Mok/PA Archive/Press Association Images
p20: Yui Mok/PA Archive/Press Association Images
p21: Yui Mok/PA Archive/Press Association Images
p23: Matt Crossick/EMPICS Entertainment
p24: Ian West/PA Archive/Press Association Images
p25: MATT DUNHAM/AP/Press Association Images
p26-27: Victor R. Caivano/AP/Press Association Images
p29: Ian West/PA Wire/Press Association Images
Doug Peters/Doug Peters/EMPICS Entertainment
p31: Yui Mok/PA Archive/Press Association Images
p32: Suzan/EMPICS Entertainment
p33: Yui Mok/PA Archive/Press Association Images
p34: Lefteris Pitarakis/AP/Press Association Images
p35: Suzan/EMPICS Entertainment
p36: Nabor Goulart/AP/Press Association Images
p37: Victor R. Caivano/AP/Press Association Images
p39: Richard Drew/AP/Press Association Images
Yui Mok/PA Wire/Press Association Images
p41: Fiona Hanson/PA Archive/Press Association Images
p42: Ian West/PA Archive/Press Association Images
p43: AFF/UK Press/Press Association Images
p44: Yui Mok/PA Wire/Press Association Images
p45: Chicago/Chicago/EMPICS Entertainment
p47: Suzan/EMPICS Entertainment
p48-49: Joel Ryan/AP/Press Association Images
p51: Peter Kramer/AP/Press Association Images
Gorassini Giancarlo/ABACA/Press Association Images
p53: Yui Mok/PA Wire/Press Association Images
p54: Brian Kersey/AP/Press Association Images

p55: Justin Goff/UK Press/Press Association Images
p56: Matt Dunham/AP/Press Association Images
p59: Ian West/PA Wire/Press Association Images
JK/allaction.co.uk /EMPICS Entertainment
p61: Steven Governo/AP/Press Association Images
p62: Chicago/Chicago/EMPICS Entertainment
Kevork Djansezian/AP/Press Association Images
Roy Catherall/Roy Catherall/Press Association Images
p63: Joel Ryan/AP/Press Association Images
p64: Chicago/Chicago/EMPICS Entertainment
p65: Chicago/Chicago/EMPICS Entertainment
p66: AP/Press Association Images
p67: Stefan Rousseau/PA Archive/Press Association Images
p68-69: Anthony Devlin/PA Archive/Press Association Images
p71: Ian West/PA Archive/Press Association Images
Ian West/PA Archive/Press Association Images
p73: Suzan/EMPICS Entertainment
p75: Yui Mok/PA Archive/Press Association Images
p76: Doug Peters/Doug Peters/EMPICS Entertainment
p77: Mark Cuthbert/UK Press/Press Association Images
p79: Roy Catherall/Roy Catherall/Press Association Images
p81: Dennis Van Tine/ABACA USA/Empics Entertainment
L6026D/UK Press/Press Association Images
p83: Matt Crossick/EMPICS Entertainment
p84: Dominic Lipinski/PA Wire/Press Association Images
p85: Sean Dempsey/PA Wire/Press Association Images
p86: Kirsty Wigglesworth/AP/Press Association Images
p87: John Phillips/UK Press/Press Association Images
Lefteris Pitarakis/AP/Press Association Images
Lefteris Pitarakis/AP/Press Association Images
p89: Anonymous/AP/Press Association Images
PA/PA Wire/Press Association Images
All Action/EMPICS Entertainment
AP/AP/Press Association Images
p91: Rowan Miles/EMPICS Entertainment
Ian West/PA Wire/Press Association Images
p92-93: Lefteris Pitarakis/AP/Press Association Images
p95: Suzan/EMPICS Entertainment
Sean Dempsey/PA Wire/Press Association Images
Back cover: Yui Mok/PA Wire/Press Association Images
Alexandre Severo/AP/Press Association Images
Matt Dunham/AP/Press Association Images
Javarman/Shutterstock.com